Head Over Heels

Astoria Wright

A Sassy Sleuth Mystery

Book 2

Head Over Heels

Copyright © 2019 by Astoria Wright

Published by Novelwright Press, LLC
Novelwright.com

Cover Art by James from GoOnWrite
GoOnWrite.com

Edited by 529 Books
529books.com

NOVELWRIGHT
PRESS, LLC

Table of Contents

Chapter 1

Beauty Rest 1

Chapter 2

Dressed to Kill...9

Chapter 3

Skin Deep.. 15

Chapter 4

Ventures in Vanity 23

Chapter 5

Not a Hair out of Place... 35

Chapter 6

Victress Cosmetics.. 42

Chapter 7

Drop Dead Gorgeous... 55

Chapter 8

Under Her Skin 72

Chapter 9

All Made Up... 80

Chapter 10

Smoke and Mirrors.. 85

Chapter 11

Concealer 91

Chapter 12

Eye of the Beholder.. 98

Chapter 13

A Turn on the Catwalk 108

Chapter 14

A Thing of Beauty.. 113

Chapter 1

Beauty Rest

Customers chatted excitedly outside Coraline's department store. I arrived just in time to hear the hush fall over the crowd of spring shoppers. A woman in a black dress and a gold name tag pulled the bars back and unlocked the sliding doors. Sensing the eager shoppers, she parted the glass doors and let the crowd disperse through the racks of colorful clothing and accessories.

The largest retailer to grace the Blue Diamond Mall with its rent, Coraline's first day of business was set to be the grandest store opening in Diamond Springs' town history. It was also launch day for Victress Cosmetics. I had come to support its creator and my longtime friend, Victoria, who, at twenty-nine, had created a company that was, I believed, months away from making millions.

Astoria Wright

"Welcome." A woman handing out opening day coupons thrusted a wine-red paper into my hands.

"Thanks," I replied, barely registering the words *free makeover* and slipping the coupon into my purse. I continued past the power suits, confident that my pink-rose pantsuit and lavender trench coat stood out from the designs on the sales racks.

Celebratory displays filled the aisles, and heart-shaped balloons floated over the silver shelves as I passed the women's clothing and shoe departments. Perfume wafted under my nose just as I saw the cosmetics counters sitting in front of the mall entrance. Customers trickled in, including Victoria Jelant.

I waved. Victoria's bronzed face lit up with a megawatt smile as she opened her arms to greet me. My straight, blonde hair met her raven-black curls as we embraced. Her stunning cerulean pantsuit matched perfectly with her mustard belt and purse. She was five years my senior, but the years only showed in the elegance of her wardrobe.

Suddenly, Victoria turned her head and I followed her line of vision. A middle-aged woman in a daffodil dress and sandals was entering the store. She shifted her eyes toward the display next to us at the entrance.

Head Over Heels

I read the sign as well. "'*Victress: For a Winning Complexion.*' I love it! I tried out the testers you sent me."

"What did you think?" Victoria glanced at me and then back at the woman.

"It's my new favorite brand." I tilted my head so she could see the Light Luminary foundation and the Queen Pink eye shadow around my green eyes. All of Victress's products had exquisite names, such as Victoria's own shade of foundation, Earth Empress, which matched her perfectly.

She smiled. "Thanks. Now all I need is for the customers to love it as much as you do."

"How could they not?" I asked.

Victoria pulled me away from the counter. "It might help if we weren't standing in front of the product."

I admired the Victress samples. The rose gold containers with the glittery symbols came in an assortment of lipsticks, glosses, blushes, foundations, and even a brush set.

The middle-aged woman neared. I stepped aside. As the woman perused the perfumes stamped with the curvy Victress "V," I shared a smile with Victoria.

Joining her at the counter, I remarked, "It's definitely eye-catching."

"That's the goal." Victoria adjusted store signs as we walked around the makeup department. Anything crooked wouldn't pass Victoria's standards. She had an eye for detail and kept glancing at the woman who was currently examining her makeup.

"How long is the trial period before they sign for a nation-wide contract?" I asked.

"Six months. Then, when sales here show promise, Victress Cosmetics will be available at Coraline department stores everywhere."

The way she said "when" filled me with joy. If anything ensured her success, it was her confidence in the quality of her products. I put an arm around her shoulders and pulled her into a side hug, saying, "I'm so happy for you!"

Victoria felt tense. I let go and gave her a sympathetic look.

"Nervous?" I asked, fully aware that even if she were, Victoria would never admit it.

"Are you nervous about your date tonight?" she deflected.

"The blind date Scarlett told me I was going on without giving me a choice?"

"You've been back in town for three months and the only man I've seen you near is Ace. Scarlett's right, you should put yourself out there. Unless Ace has your attention?"

"He's my boss. And I'm always with him because we're always working a case. It seems like everyone needs a private investigator for some reason or another." Changing subjects, I added, "I haven't seen you going on any dates lately. You're just as much a workaholic as I am—more, I think."

"I'm building a business. Besides, I haven't had a godmother who knows me inside out helping me navigate the narrow pool of suitors in Diamond Springs. I can imagine the men you've dated as a model, and those diamonds in the rough are rare in this town. If Scarlett thinks she found a guy for you, I say go for it."

I couldn't picture what Victoria viewed as a good catch. Even when she was working at a mall cart outside of a jewelry store, Victoria had been killing it as a small business owner. She had a body toned with self-defense classes and dancercises, a mind sharpened by business seminars and experience, and a personality strengthened by a strong work ethic and a no-nonsense attitude. And she had no tolerance for drama.

"I can't just watch for potential sales all day. Since we're speaking of Scarlett, how about breakfast and a coffee at Sycamore Bookstore?"

"Absolutely," I said. I had seen Scarlett Sycamore often but hadn't been in her bookshop, Sycamore's, for at least a month.

Business had finally begun to slow down for us, which is how I even had the time to meet Victoria today. I had been looking forward to a little reprieve.

I turned to follow Victoria into the mall when the browsing customer she'd been watching out of the corner of her eye began complaining.

"No, I'm not interested in a makeover. Do I look like I need one?"

"May I offer you a spritz of the Victress perfume?" the saleswoman asked while proceeding to spray.

"Get that out of my face." The customer coughed and waved her hand wildly.

"What's going on?" A saleswoman in the same type of lab coat, dark hair, and too much makeup appeared.

Victoria and I walked closer to the customer while we watched this woman berate her associate.

"Daisy, that's two of the same testers you've opened, and you've disturbed a customer."

"I'm sorry," the nervous saleswoman fumbled as she stuffed the sample perfume back into its box.

The woman, whom I now realized was the manager, took a paper out of the outer pocket of her lab coat. "I'm very sorry, ma'am. Here, please take a voucher for a—ma'am?"

The customer stumbled, clutching the counter instead of the coupon. She swayed as if the world had moved under her feet. The young saleswoman's hands began to shake. She dropped the box. Then she knocked over several others as she clumsily stooped to pick it up. The sound of falling merchandise turned some heads, but the woman's raspy breathing led Victoria and I to the woman's side.

"Are you all right?" Victoria asked.

The manager, who had bent to help Daisy, bolted upright, saying, "Just leave the bottles." She stepped around Daisy, walking to the counter opposite her toward a phone.

The customer bent forward, heaving so hard she had to grasp the counter. Her face reddened unnaturally and swelled.

"Hives?" Victoria asked.

I shook my head. I dared not say *"no, it's far worse,"* while the woman could hear me. I placed my hand on the woman's back and left shoulder, trying to hold her up. Victoria gripped her right arm to steady her.

"Ma'am?" I uttered.

Astoria Wright

The woman collapsed. She grasped at her chest as she fell. The chain of her necklace snapped, sending pearls in every direction. The saleswoman gasped. A hush fell over the shoppers who had huddled around us.

"Call 911. Quick!" Victoria shouted.

"They're on their way, hold on," said the manager with the phone pressed to her ear.

Through shaky breath, the injured woman wheezed her last words: "She's killed me."

Chapter 2

Dressed to Kill

Ace answered his phone with a gravelly "hello?" It was early in the morning for a Saturday, but I classified this as an emergency.

"How fast can you get down to the Blue Diamond Mall?"

"Kait? I don't know, twenty minutes, I guess. What's wrong?"

"Meet me at Coraline's for a new investigation."

"You took on a case? Kait, you know I have three on my desk already."

"We've been handling five at a time for weeks, Ace. And a cheating spouse and two background checks are not as important as murder."

"Murder? Who?"

"I'll tell you everything when you get here." I ended the call and went back to Victoria, who was more shaken than I'd ever seen her.

"Are you all right?" I asked.

Victoria's eyes remained on the victim as paramedics lifted her onto a stretcher. I swallowed the lump in my throat. The woman had died just before the paramedics had arrived. By then she'd looked like a burn victim, red and puffy with lesions on her forearms.

"I'm so sorry this happened on today of all days," I said.

"It's not that." Victoria shifted her gaze to the counter, where the woman who had sprayed the perfume was explaining what had happened to the police. I recognized Officers Hart and Jones from a previous encounter when they'd accused my friend, Ava Price, of murdering a woman who'd shoplifted from her shoe store, Sensational Soles. Jones rummaged through the bottles on the shelves as the woman showed Hart the product she'd used on the customer. I had a sneaking suspicion they'd point the finger at a friend of mine again.

"It wasn't the perfume," Victoria said, when Hart walked over to us. I couldn't imagine Victoria's products had anything to do with this woman's death. But I knew for certain that if the police so much as hinted that it did,

Victoria's career might be killed. I put a hand on her forearm, hoping she'd get the hint not to say anything else.

Jasper Hart tilted his head. "Is there a particular reason you think I'd suspect the perfume?"

"Maybe that," I said, letting go of Victoria's arm and lifting my chin toward Jones. As he questioned Daisy, Jones held the box with the assaulting perfume inside.

Hart's frown was followed by the words, "Standard procedure. What was your name, Miss?"

Victoria held her head high. "I'm the owner of Victress Cosmetics." She reached for a purse that was no longer on her arm. Looking around, we spotted her oversized yellow leather bag on the floor near where the victim had lain. I picked it up and nearly dropped it. She used to carry samples with her when she was first starting her business and, judging by the weight, she still did.

Victoria rifled through the bag, handing Hart her business card.

Hart raised an eyebrow. "You're the one who made the perfume that may have killed Mrs. LeBeau?"

Now I had the victim's name. But I didn't like the way he phrased her death or the tone in which he said it.

I put a hand on my hip. "You don't know that's what killed her."

"I said 'may have.' We'll have a lab report by the end of the day, though. I understand you two were with her when she passed?"

Victoria and I recounted near-identical versions of what had happened. Hart wrote it all in his notebook, nodding occasionally or murmuring "mmhmm" as if he'd doubt us if we told him the sky was blue. At the end of it, he looked each of us in the eye.

"Was there anything else, anything you noticed that was suspicious?"

I swallowed and clenched my jaw. Mrs. LeBeau's accusation had come out as barely a whisper. I might not have understood her correctly, and if I had, she clearly meant Daisy. But the officers might interpret that as Victoria had killed her.

Before I could respond, Victoria said, "No, I don't think so."

Hart left it at that, clicking his pen and nodding. "Appreciate your cooperation. If we have further questions, we'll contact you. In the meantime, I advise you not to leave town."

"Am I a suspect?" Victoria asked.

"We haven't confirmed that it is murder, Miss Jelant. It's too early to say anything."

I fought the urge to roll my eyes. He'd as much as accused Victoria, no matter what he said now. I waited for him to leave and then turned to Victoria, who turned to exit Coraline's. Near a cupcake cart just outside Coraline's, Victoria plopped her bag onto a chair and sat. Placing her elbows on a table, she rested her head in her hands. She'd gone three shades paler.

I sat opposite her. "Don't worry about Hart. Ace and I are going to be in on the investigation."

"You are?" Victoria looked at me with hope.

My chest tightened. I'd never seen her like this. "I want to help. But, if there's any information you have about Mrs. LeBeau's death, you have to tell me."

Victoria snatched her bag up. "Not here. We need to go somewhere private."

"You wanted lunch at Sycamore's? Ace could join us there." I suggested.

Scarlett Sycamore kept a table reserved for friends and family in the back of the café of her bookstore. As my godmother, she wouldn't mind me taking up the space whenever I needed it. And I needed it now more than ever.

"Perfect," Victoria said. "Once we're there, I'll tell you everything."

Chapter 3
Skin Deep

Sycamore Bookstore had made some improvements since November. As any chain store, it still retained a cozy feel. The layout began with a well-stocked children's section, including a stage area for read-alongs and a giant tree-shaped bookcase. The rest of store contained a fair amount of mystery, science fiction, and fantasy books. Non-fiction and memoirs held the interest of Scarlett's monthly book club meetings.

At the very back, I found the scent of freshly brewed coffee in the café section comforting. Victoria inhaled the aroma and let out a long breath.

Tucked into a far corner table with our sandwiches and coffees, Victoria finally felt comfortable enough to speak. "I knew Mrs. LeBeau, you probably guessed that already. She was a customer of mine when I owned the cart outside Zazbry's."

Ace took a sip of his black coffee. "I remember the cart, vaguely. It was cosmetics at that time, too, wasn't it?"

Victoria nodded. "Sally LeBeau was really nice at first. She came by the cart regularly. Then she started lodging complaints about everything."

"What kind of complaints?" Ace tapped his pen against his notepad. I'd worked with him long enough to know that he was putting together a theory as he did that. So early into her story, that wasn't a good sign.

"It was little things—the foundation colors I mixed, the perfumes leaving an unpleasant after-scent. Then, she said my perfume had given her hives. I told her that my products were tested and that wasn't possible. None of it was true—she even admitted later that a doctor had said it was a stress-related breakout. But then she came back to complain about how I'd handled it. She said I shouldn't own a store at all and if it was up to her I'd be tossed out of the mall."

"What happened after that?" Ace asked.

"I called security. She was unreasonable. Eventually, the mall manager had to get involved. Of course, Sally went in on Ella Belle, too. The one good thing is that since I defended Ella, she's been nicer to me. It's good having a mall manager on your side, especially when a shopper swears to get you shut down."

"It sounds like she should've been banned by the mall," I said.

"That's what you would think. But I found out from some of the other cart owners that Sally was a mystery shopper. She wasn't just lodging complaints willy-nilly. She was hired by the mall and Ella's superiors said they couldn't ban her for making complaints."

"Sorry, what's a mystery shopper?" Ace asked.

"A person who's hired to test a company's service," I explained.

"We're not supposed to know who they are, but somehow one of the shop owners figured it out."

"But you were not part of a larger store. Why would she test you?" I asked.

"I was applying for my makeup line to take a spot in Coraline's department store, so they might have hired her. Or it might've been a marketing agency. Blue Diamond Mall hires them for general assessment of the mall and its stores. I suspected the latter because of the way she insisted on seeing the mall director. But then we saw her in Coraline's today." Victoria shrugged.

I said, "So, she might have been in Coraline's as a mystery shopper. But Sally wasn't interested in any of your products."

Victoria sighed. "I saw that and I was relieved at first. But then the girl at the counter—she was trying way too hard at her job, probably because she knew Sally was a mystery shopper."

I had wondered why Daisy had insisted on the perfume. Pushiness was the stereotype of salespeople at cosmetics counters, which is probably why I'd brushed that off. But I'd found that not to be the case in general.

"I think we need to question the saleswoman," I said.

"I agree." Ace shut the notebook and did his dreaded stare down. Locking eyes with Victoria, he stood, reached a hand out, and said, "We may stop by your place of business later. I hope you'll have some time to see us, Miss Jelant."

Victoria stood and shook Ace's hand. "Of course, here, take my card," Victoria let go and rifled through her purse. I stood, coming close enough to see her eyes bulge for a split-second. Before I could ask what was wrong, Victoria shut the bag and chuckled.

"I seem to be out of cards. Kait knows my information, so she can tell you all that, right?"

I glanced at Ace, hoping he had missed the break in her smile and her shallow breathing. Trying to pretend I hadn't seen anything, I nodded my head and smiled.

Victoria walked away with determined steps. Ace stepped so close behind me he might as well have been breathing down my neck. I froze, my feelings for Ace stirred by the scent of his sea breeze cologne. But when I turned around, Ace's eyes were tracing Victoria with hawk-like intensity. I frowned.

"You suspect her, don't you?"

"If it is murder, she did just give us a motive." His eyes softened as he looked at me. "Of course, it's always possible it was just an accidental death. Based on what Victoria said, LeBeau was susceptible to allergic reactions."

"You think so?" I wanted to breathe a sigh of relief, but I sank into thought. In my mind, I heard the woman's last words *"she's killed me"* and reinterpreted their meaning. If she did have some kind of life-threatening allergy, she might have meant that Daisy's spray had provoked the allergy. "That would explain it," I thought out loud.

I caught Ace's gray eyes.

"What?" I asked.

He crossed his arms. "Is there something you're not telling me?"

I sighed, confessing that I hadn't told the officers her last words. I expected Ace to relax, smile, and agree with me that no harm was done in leaving that out of my summation for the police. Instead, his expression turned cross and his arms remained folded.

"You shouldn't have left that out. Withholding information is a crime."

"Sorry. I thought the police might mistake her meaning and blame Victoria."

"That wasn't for you to decide," Ace said.

I had no argument. "I can tell them next time I see them. It won't make a difference, though. Mrs. LeBeau clearly meant Daisy had accidentally triggered her allergies. I'm sure of it."

Ace's lips twisted into a conflicted frown.

"What?" I asked.

"That information might change Hart's mind. Plus, I hate to say it, but Victoria did act like she might have something to hide."

My eyes flared. Ace held a hand up. "I'm not making any accusations. Let's just talk to the saleswoman. Agreed?"

Head Over Heels

I grabbed my purse off the table so hard I almost pulled the strap clear off. Then, I bumped into Ace again. He hadn't walked farther into the store, as I'd expected. His back was turned to me as he looked around the bookstore.

"What is it?" I snapped.

"Isn't Scarlett usually here?"

"You know Scarlett Sycamore?" My anger shifted to annoyed curiosity.

"Since childhood. I used to come to this bookstore with my sister all the time."

I knew Ace was only six years my senior. I'd helped his sister, Maisie, with the plans for his upcoming thirtieth birthday party. But I thought of him as a distinguished gentleman—timeless in a way. His lack of a social media presence and disdain for technology might have shaped my view of him. Even meeting his sister was a surprise starting with a message that came out of nowhere asking me to be friends – on Facebook of all the social media platforms.

That was her only social media presence since she preferred face-to-face meetings. Though we'd only met a handful of times, she was so warm and friendly I felt like we had known each other forever. I hadn't realized that she and Ace had known Scarlett, too.

Astoria Wright

"Did you need to see Scarlett now?" I realized as I asked it that I needed to see Scarlett myself—to tell her that I couldn't make the lunch with my blind date. Then again, if the questioning didn't take long, I might still make it within the hour.

Ace shook his head. "Never mind, we don't have time to see her. We have an overzealous saleswoman to question."

Chapter 4
Ventures in Vanity

Daisy Greenbent had gone home with a headache. I suspected her true diagnosis was a guilty conscious. According to her department manager, Lottie Hambledon, she'd been crying nonstop since the incident and had to be sent home.

The salespeople still on the floor tried their best to smile through the day, as Ella Belle wouldn't let Coraline's close down on their first day of business. The yellow tape cordoning off Daisy's station attracted less customers than curious passersby. I doubted it would help business any, but then, I wasn't a shrewd business woman with a heart of stone like Ella.

Speaking of the devil, Ella sauntered up to the counter where we were questioning Lottie and touched Ace's sleeve. She barely looked at me, except when Ace stepped back as if to remind her I was there. Then she gave me a poor you look.

"I realize how distressing it must've been for you to witness a murder on the launch day of your friend's makeup line."

I gave her as much pseudo-concern back. "And I can imagine how concerning it is for you as the Blue Diamond Mall manager to have had two murders here within months of each other."

Ace's eyes shifted from her to me. "Kait and I aren't ruling out other possibilities yet, Ella. This might not be murder."

Ella's smile was triumphant as she hooked her arm around Ace's. "I'm glad to hear you say that. Actually, I was hoping to talk to you about Mrs. LeBeau's death," she said as she dragged him away.

I must have had contempt written all over my face, because Lottie leaned over the counter, saying, "I understand how you feel."

"What?" I took a moment to snap out of my distain.

"About Ella. She's a devil in whatever color pantsuit she's wearing any given day."

Lottie spoke with such venom I found it hard to imagine disliking anyone that much. Granted, it was

Ella, but even she had her redeeming qualities. I tilted my head curiously.

"Does everyone think that of her?"

Lottie shrugged. "I have yet to meet a store manager who likes her—except maybe the ones who kiss up to her. What's she done to you, besides the obvious?"

"What do you mean?"

Lottie looked pointedly at her and Ace. The mischievous look in her eye told me she thought Ella had stolen more than Ace's attention. I shook my head, a little too fervently.

"Oh no, he's my boss and she's just an acquaintance. He knows all the local business people, just in case he ever needs information. Ace likes to have as many contacts as he can."

"He's having a whole lot of contact right now."

I couldn't help but follow her gaze. I was not surprised to see Ella repeatedly touching Ace's wrist and shoulder. The briefest glance at me revealed her game.

She wasn't interested in a man like Ace. I knew her type and it was more show than substance. Ace was handsome in a scruffy, tall, dark and mysterious way, but she'd always gone after the model type. My ex-boyfriend type. In fact, she had gone after an ex before, who had the good sense to turn her down and tell me about it. This display with Ace was purely for my provocation.

I wasn't the least bit worried. Not that Ella wasn't attractive enough with her tall, slender, red-haired, fair-skinned physique to lure a man into her lap. The bait was alluring to most men. But her current prey wasn't like most men. Ace wouldn't fall for her. I was as sure of that as I was of my growing attraction to him. I pushed that thought aside pronto and cross-examined Lottie.

"So, what did Ella do to you to make you so angry at her?" I asked. My eyes kept darting to Ella and Ace. As much as I wasn't worried, I didn't like her throwing herself at him that way.

"What didn't she do? If she likes you, you're made, but if she doesn't like you, she can unmake everything you've built in a second." Lottie stiffened. A sudden wide-eyed look came over her and she hid it by batting her eyes and smiling. "I mean, that's what I hear from my coworkers around the mall."

From what I heard in her voice, she meant something different than what she was saying. But I couldn't tell exactly what. And I couldn't tell if she was hiding something for herself or for someone else. Whatever it was, that was all I was going to get out of Lottie before Ella rejoined us.

Head Over Heels

"Thank you, Ace, but the compliments are really unnecessary. Lottie, I think we've held the workers here long enough after such a troubling day. The officers wanted us to keep people away from the crime scene, anyway. I think it's best to just let everyone from the store go home now. We'll do a relaunch of the grand opening in a week."

"Generous," I said, knowing full well that any other sane person would have closed the store immediately. Still, it was a shock that Ella had reversed a decision. "What changed your mind?"

She hooked Ace's arm. "I could never disagree with this man. He always makes a good point. It really was brave of the store workers to soldier on, but since there is a possibility this wasn't a natural death, I think it's best to shut everything down for the time being."

Pulling his arm away but hiding the discomfort I knew he must be feeling, Ace held her hands and smiled. "A wise decision. Ella, if you wouldn't mind, we'd like to ask Ms. Hambledon a few questions."

"Be my guest." She turned to me. "Kait, take care of yourself. Your eyes look a little puffy."

"Don't worry about me, Ella. You can't afford the wrinkles."

I didn't like this catty part of myself, but I couldn't help it.

Brushing my arm as she walked past, Ella muttered, "You have ten minutes before security has to close up the shop."

With that delightful threat, Ella Belle left the store. Fortunately, Ace didn't waste time. He jumped right into the questioning, with his notebook in hand.

"Now, Ms. Hambledon—"

"It's Miss," Lottie corrected.

From the way her eyes darted from Ace to me and to Ella, who was still within earshot, I knew she had no qualms about getting in on the fight for Ace's affection. I almost rolled my eyes. It didn't matter. Ace was oblivious, flipping through his notebook to find an empty page. At least, I kept telling myself that.

"I noticed that you have two selections of perfumes from Victress Cosmetics."

"That's right." She walked with us toward the counter. Without disturbing the yellow tape, she pointed, explaining, "Winning Spirit and Winning Essence. It's essentially the same scent, but the essence is the lighter of the two."

"The bottles look identical to me," Ace said.

Head Over Heels

The perfumes were both in black bottles with diamond toppers. The largest symbol was the vertical letters for VICTRESS, while the perfume titles were listed sideways along the brand in smaller letters. To amateur eyes, the two might have looked the same. Perhaps it had to the police as well.

But my skill in fashion gave me a leg up. "The font color is a fuchsia on the Spirit and magenta on the Essence, and, of course, the titles are different."

"Which one was sprayed on Mrs. LeBeau?" Ace asked.

"The Spirit. The tester was taken by the police," Lottie answered.

"What about the tester for the Essence?" I asked. I didn't see one on the counter.

"I don't think we received one."

"Is that unusual?" Ace asked.

Lottie's lips dipped. "Not necessarily. Some companies do that, especially since it was a lighter version of the other perfume."

I raised an eyebrow. That didn't sound right to me. I'd been in numerous cosmetics shops since I was a child and I remembered seeing every scent in stock on the shelves of most stores. It might not have been unheard of for a company to leave out a tester or even for an error to be made in a shipment, but Victoria was not one to make mistakes. Ace caught on to another abnormality in Lottie's story.

"You said you don't 'think' you received any of those testers. Wouldn't you have that on record?"

Lottie walked back to her own counter and retrieved a clipboard for Ace and me to read. It was a shipment tracking form. On the line for the Victress shipment was Daisy Greenbent's name.

"Daisy was the one who received and unpacked the shipment."

"But Daisy isn't a manager. Do regular store employees sign for shipments?" Ace asked.

"Not usually, but Daisy needed the overtime and I had to leave early a couple of times for personal reasons. I trust her."

"Did you ask her about the missing tester?" I said.

"No, why would I? I told you, sometimes companies don't include testers."

"It would be on the list, though. Did the invoice say Victress would provide testers for both perfumes?" Ace asked.

Lottie flipped a few pages and traced the form with her finger. Tapping the paper and then her chin, she said, "Hmm, it does. I guess that was an oversight." She snapped the papers back and set the clipboard on the shelf beneath the counter. "There has been a lot to do in the last few weeks. Store openings wouldn't be 'grand' if they were so easy. I can't be responsible for everything."

"It happens," Ace reassured. He looked down at his notepad and scribbled furiously—a good sign. "Where were you when Daisy sprayed Mrs. LeBeau with the perfume?"

"I was here, at this counter."

"So you saw the spraying?" he asked without looking up at her.

I tried to contain my smile. She was sounding more and more suspect.

"Maybe from the corner of my eye. I had my own customers to watch over."

"You went over to her counter after Mrs. LeBeau shouted, though, didn't you?" I challenged.

Lottie pressed her lips into a thin line. "It's my job to handle customer complaints."

"What did you do when LeBeau fell?" Ace asked.

"I was helping Daisy. Her hands were shaking so much she dropped the tester."

"Did you pick it up?"

"I don't think so, maybe I handed it to her. I told the police I don't remember. It happened so fast."

"What did you do next? Were you near Mrs. LeBeau?"

Lottie shifted her weight from one foot to the other. "No." She looked at me. "You and the woman with you. You were near her. I was calling an ambulance."

My mouth opened, ready to protest the tone of voice with which she was making her thinly veiled accusation.

Ace interrupted me before I could speak. "Thank you for your time, Miss Hambledon."

I added, "Make sure you stay in town. We'll be in touch."

Ace nodded and smiled as we walked away. A few steps from the exit, he said, "What was that? You're telling people to stay in town now?"

"You would have said it if I hadn't. She's clearly a suspect," I said.

"Miss Hambledon is a witness. She's not suspected of anything."

"But Victoria is?"

"I never said," he started. Then he recounted it, "You know what? Yes. If the perfume was poisoned, she'd be a suspect sooner or later. I know how police minds work. We might as well accept that as a possibility and not let our emotions bias us on this case."

Head Over Heels

If my face wasn't red and steam wasn't billowing out of my ears, then my green eyes had to at least be glowing. "Easy for you since you don't seem to have any emotions. I do and I don't care if I'm biased, I know Victoria and I'm telling you she didn't do this. Lottie should be a suspect. So should Daisy for that matter. Both had access to the crime scene and the murder weapon."

"Kait, please try to understand. I can't rule anything out. Including the possibility that this is not murder. You told me you took this job to become my partner one day; if you really want to do that, you have to start acting like a P.I."

I was surprised he remembered the off-handed comment I'd made when he'd first hired me. I hadn't exactly said I wanted to be a P.I., only that I'd rather be called an executive assistant because it was one step closer to partner than if he'd thought of me as his secretary. Part of me wasn't sure if I'd meant partner in the workplace sense or a romantic one.

I let the thought escape in an inhale-exhale breathing exercise I hoped Ace would interpret as me letting go of my anger. "Okay, but we should start with Daisy."

Ace nodded. "I'll get Daisy's information from the police. I'd like to see the statements they collected from her first. Meanwhile, we still have those other cases.

There's no sense in both of us going down to the station. You could get those background checks done, and I'll call you with an update as soon as I can."

I knew he was just trying to keep me busy to get me out of the way, but I also know that Officer Hart didn't want private investigators in his station. He made an exception for Ace. I was discovering Ace was the exception to the rule in a lot of places around town. Even with me, since I usually didn't give in so easily.

"Fine," I said, "but no interviewing Daisy without me."

"Agreed, I'll wait for you before doing any interviewing."

While I felt a slight twinge of guilt about it, I hadn't promised him I would do the same.

Chapter 5
Not a Hair out of Place

It took a few hours to gather the information, print, and set the completed background checks on Ace's desk for him to page through old-school style. Then, since all the databases were still open in tabs on my laptop, I typed a few more names into the system. Addresses for Daisy Greenbent, Lottie Hambledon, even Sally LeBeau came up with no trouble. I scrawled Daisy's address down on a sticky note—now I was picking up Ace's old-fashioned habits—when my perfectly accessible phone vibrated inches from my fingers on the desk. I ripped the sticky off and pocketed it, then read the text that had flashed on my screen.

I heard about Victoria. Do you need to reschedule your date? Call me.

Scarlett's name appeared beside a heart emoji. My lips curved down and my fingers curled around the phone as I remembered my blind date. It was 11:20 a.m. I had less than an hour before my lunch date, but I couldn't see that going well now. I imagined a brief conversation going like this:

"How are you?"

"Fine, but I witnessed a murder at the mall today, so actually, not fine at all."

And then there was the oh-so-fun question: *"So, what do you do for a living?"*

"Thanks for asking, I help solve cases like that murder I just mentioned. In fact, I'm trying to prove my friend didn't kill that woman, but my boss thinks she did. Oh, speaking of my boss, I have a secret crush him, but don't worry, if you're everything Scarlett says you are, I'm sure I'll be just as into you."

Scarlett did make my mystery man seem like Prince Charming. In fact, she had tried to set us up once before, she'd said, when I was just out of high school and he was in college. If I hadn't chosen to pursue modeling in Europe, perhaps we would have had that blind date long ago, but now all I could remember from that time was my excitement as I prepared for my first overseas Fashion Week. I didn't recall his name and now Scarlett wouldn't tell me anything except that he was everything I'd ever said I wanted, which, at this point in my life, was really just a gentleman who knew how to treat people with kindness. Everything else was negotiable. But back when I was a teen, I may have had notions of a tall, dark, and handsome Mr. Right, and the twinkle in Scarlett's hazel eyes had told me he was all that and more. Whether or not this was true, I couldn't just stand him up.

I pressed the button to call Scarlett and headed to the door. The first ring barely finished when I heard, "Hello? Kait, are you okay?"

"Yes, I'm fine."

"I already talked to your date, and it's all right if you can't make it for lunch."

"You told him about the murder?" I turned the key and felt my stomach knot up as I locked the door.

"I didn't say a word more to him than I have to you. And I didn't tell him you're working the case. He called to say *he* couldn't make it. I figured it was for the best. When should I reschedule?"

Did I want her to reschedule? I scratched my forehead with my key. Then I spun around, clicker in hand, and unlocked my car door.

"I don't think right now is a good ti—"

"How about tonight at 7:00 p.m.? A dinner is better than a lunch anyway," Scarlett said.

"Really, Scarlett, I—"

"Unless a Sunday brunch tomorrow works better for you?"

"No, dinner is better, but—"

"Perfect. I'll tell him that time works for you. Listen, I just got to the bookstore, so I have to go. We'll talk later. Good luck with Victoria's case."

I let out a groan and walked three steps to my car. Stopping just at the curb, I noticed my text messages were still open and I realized I'd missed a text from this morning.

I had to do a double take on the sender's name: Cosima Shine. I never did know for certain whether that was her real name or one she'd chosen for her modeling career, but I could picture my old friend typing away on the keyboard in her makeup chair between shoots to fit in time for her friends. Cosima redefined efficiency, which is why a text from her was always abrupt and to the point: *Did Helen call you?*

Helen Teagan, I assumed. My old agent and discoverer had tried to rope me back into a resort show this spring, but that was via letter back in November. I hadn't heard from her since.

Head Over Heels

I texted back: *No, why?*

Figuring she'd get back to me later, I nearly pocketed the phone, but it buzzed in my hand. A second text from Cosima appeared on the screen.

Call 2night. 6:00 p.m.

That meant she'd call me. Since I had a date tonight, the 6:00 p.m. timing brought an under-the-breath "ugh" to my lips, but since I knew that was possibly her only free moment, I texted an *OK* back. Then I placed the phone into my purse, made my way for the car, and promptly stopped as Ace's four-door Hyundai pulled into the spot next to my Bentley. He gave me a crooked smile complete with that annoying eyebrow raise. The whole look screamed *caught you* as he opened his car door.

"Daisy's not at home if that's where you're going."

My smile was too sweet. "Don't trust me?"

"With my life. But I also know you. I told you we'd question Daisy together."

"Witnesses misremember the longer the timespan between the crime and the questioning," I retorted.

"So long as you remember she is a witness, not a suspect."

"What happened to your open mind about that?" I asked.

"The possibility became a little slimmer when Daisy checked into the hospital."

"She's in the hospital?"

"Observation. She had some shortness of breath and abdominal pain. Turns out she inhaled a little of what she sprayed on Mrs. LeBeau. The symptoms appeared to be mild."

"So, the perfume *was* poisoned?"

Ace walked around to the other side of the car. "Ah, no. The bottle tested negative. Nothing toxic in it."

"Then how did Daisy Greenbent and Sally LeBeau both end up poisoned?"

He opened the passenger door. "That's a question I'm hoping we can get answered at our next destination."

I made my way to the passenger seat. "Where are we going?"

He gestured for me to sit, then swung the door closed and jogged around to take his place in the driver's seat. Once we were on our way, he said, "Turns out Daisy interviewed for a job at a startup cosmetics company."

"Really, which one?" I grinned. A competing company might mean sabotage. But would a company really go as far as murder to frame a competitor?

"The one we're going to right now, but, Kait, you're not going to like it."

That erased my grin. "It's Victress, isn't it?"

Chapter 6

Victress Cosmetics

Victress Cosmetics' headquarters took up half a floor of an office building located just outside Diamond Springs. The executive suite consisted of a modest lobby, a conference room, two cosmetics labs, a storage/shipping room, and Victoria's office. It was a fantastic set-up and one I knew hinged on a massive loan her flawless business plan had earned her from the local bank.

Victoria was not one of my boarding school friends. Instead, she was a born and raised Diamond Springs sensation, with a mind sharper than a diamond's edge. So, I wasn't surprised to hear that Victoria was on a conference call with a potential client from a boutique store with interest in carrying her brand. Her secretary, Noah, showed us Victoria's schedule.

Head Over Heels

"She has several small clients and two meetings with franchises looking to stock her brand. One is Raina Boutique, whom she's on the line with right now, and another with a subscription service, Boxed & Beautiful. That was for next week."

"Was?" I asked.

"Is. Well, was." Noah's shoulders tensed, then he shrugged. "They called today saying they'd have to reschedule but didn't know when."

Ace gestured toward Noah's tablet and he handed it over. The exchange kept Ace from seeing my frustration. "I thought you said the police weren't going to publicize anything until they made an arrest."

While tapping screens, Ace replied, "Small towns. People talk." Then, he handed the tablet back to Noah. "We'll wait." He smiled.

I didn't follow him to the chairs right away. I wasn't going to pass over a chance to see everything. I asked for the tablet instead of demanding it. Noah met my eyes with a pleasant smile as he handed it to me. I briefly wondered if my blind date would have piercing blue irises like Noah's. Ace's stormy gray orbs came to mind unbidden. I blinked the image away and focused on the list.

Meetings and a shipment record were all I found. Nothing out of the ordinary. It was mostly small clients, individuals who had ordered via the Victress website. Then my eye spotted the name that made me smile. Ella Belle ordered an eye shadow, some foundation, and a perfume.

Either some of the old Ella still existed beneath the surface that knew how to be supportive of old friends, or Victoria's product was just that good. I assumed the latter. Still, other than the order from Coraline's, there was nothing on the list that connected Victoria to today's murder. One thing stood out, though.

I tapped the screen to zoom in on the name of the manager who'd placed the order and the employee who'd signed off on delivery. Then, I handed it to Ace.

"Lottie Hambledon placed the order?"

Ace nodded. "And Daisy signed for it. That all lines up with what Lottie told us."

I asked Noah, "Do you remember a woman named Daisy Greenbent? Roughly 5'3," short brown hair, excellent color-coordination skills. She would have come in about a week ago regarding a job."

"Sorry. That describes a lot of the applicants."

"Did you have many?" Ace asked.

"At least a dozen."

"Any of them stand out?" I asked.

He began to shake his head, then paused and looked at me. "Wait, yeah, there was one. She wasn't an applicant, though."

The outer door opened and in stepped Officers Hart and Jones. Hart rolled his eyes when he saw us but was polite enough to tip his head. "Ace. Kait. I see you beat us here."

Ace smiled. "Only by a few seconds. We were just asking Noah a few questions."

"Which ones did I miss?" Hart asked while Jones showed Noah a search warrant. Hart nodded and Jones headed straight for the cosmetics lab.

Ace and Hart stepped aside, scrolling through the tablet to bring him up to speed.

"You were telling us about a woman?" I reminded Noah.

"Yeah, there was a woman here late one night. It had to be around 8:00 o'clock. I had just shut down the computer and I went in the back to make sure everything was locked up when I saw a woman in the storage room. When I asked what she was doing there, all she said was 'goodnight' and she walked off in a hurry."

"Was it one of the lab workers?"

"No."

Ace walked up to the counter, drawn in to the conversation.

Hart followed, asking, "Could it have been Victoria Jelant?"

"No, I don't think so."

"You don't think it was your boss?"

Noah let out a frustrated breath. "At first, I thought it was her, since she likes to check the shipments personally, but then I remembered that Victoria left early. Plus, she didn't dress like Victoria."

"Can you describe her clothing?" Hart asked.

"She was wearing a hat and a raincoat and gloves."

The comment made Ace and Hart share a look. I knew what they were thinking. The gloves meant she could have interfered with the product.

"What was she doing?" Ace asked.

"Nothing when I saw her," Noah said.

"Did she set anything down or take anything with her?" I asked.

Noah's lips pursed, then he shook his head. "I don't think so. I didn't see a purse or anything."

"Was there anything else that might help us identify her?" Officer Hart said.

Head Over Heels

Noah put a hand through his hair. Before he'd rifled through his blond strands, his eyes widened. "Her hair. She had black hair."

"Long or short?" Ace pressed.

"I don't know. It was tucked under a hat."

I couldn't help but frown. Victoria had black hair. And with her wearing a raincoat, hat, and gloves, whoever had been in Victress headquarters did well to conceal her identity.

"You didn't try to stop her?" Hart said.

"I thought she might have been an inspector. You know, doing a surprise inspection or something."

"What made you think that?" I asked.

Noah waved us past the counter and walked us back to the shipping room. The woman would've had to pass the labs and Victoria's office to get here. The only other entrance was the fire door, clearly labeled with a red alarm will sound sign at the top.

In the shipping room, Noah flipped a switch and took a clipboard off the wall. Then he pointed toward the left wall, where a door stood ajar and muffled voices could be heard in the room behind it. The voices came from the lab next door, I surmised, which Noah confirmed.

Gesturing to door with the tip of the clipboard, he said, "That's where I entered. I made sure everything was locked up in the lab and I saw the light was on in this room, so I came in here to turn it off and lock the storage room, too. That's when I saw her with this."

Noah handed the clipboard to Ace.

He flipped through the pages. "Same information from the tablet, orders and shipping addresses."

"And the box numbers for us to place the labels when they ship out. Victoria's extremely organized."

Hart examined the list and compared them to the boxes. Noah pointed at the stacks of brown packages. He opened one right beside the officer.

Showing us the boxes of perfumes, he said, "This is what she was doing. I think she may have been examining the packaging. When I came in and saw her, she closed the box up and put the clipboard back on the wall."

"Why didn't you report any of this to me?" Victoria entered the room. Despite her heels, the carpeted hallway had muted her steps.

Noah shrugged, but he was also wincing. "I'm sorry. I thought at the time that you might have come back for something or that you had wanted to check the shipment to Coraline's yourself before it went out the next day."

"It was Coraline's shipment that this woman was inspecting?" Officer Hart asked.

"Yes, sir."

Out came Ace's notebook. I beamed. We'd found our suspect.

"So, this mysterious woman poisoned the perfumes. We find her, we find our murderer," I said.

"Did you come in to check the shipment, Ms. Jelant?" Officer Hart asked.

I opened my mouth to protest but Ace's eyes glared at me before shifting to Victoria. She crossed her arms as if she was both cold and calculating a response.

"I check the shipments when they get packaged."

"You went over that shipment personally?" Ace asked.

"Yes, before this woman broke into my storage room. It seems clear to me that Kait is right in pointing out that she's your killer."

"We'll take that into consideration, Miss Jelant, but right now I have some questions for you."

Victoria held a hand up toward the hallway. "We can go to my office." She nodded at Noah. "You can go back to the front desk." Looking at Hart, she said, "Unless you need him now?"

Officer Hart waved a hand, dismissing him. We followed Victoria and Officer Hart down the hall.

Ace remarked as we made the awkward trek to her office, "Your company seems to be taking off. I understand you went from a mall cart makeup seller to a cosmetics tycoon in a few short years. How did you manage that?"

Victoria held the door open for us with a grin. "I'm hardly a tycoon, Mr. East. I'm just a cosmetologist with a little luck and a lot of hard work."

"Either way it's impressive," Ace said.

"You're more than a cosmetologist, though. You make your own products here, don't you?" Hart asked.

Victoria sat at her desk with Hart standing beside the chairs across from her. Ace and I took the sofa by the front wall. Taking a power pose with her back against the seat, legs crossed, and her arms on the sides of the chair, Victoria appeared at ease. But I knew by the tapping finger on her desk that she was anything but relaxed.

"Not personally—not anymore. I have a cosmetic chemist who makes the products now."

"But you used to create the mixes? Are you also a cosmetic chemist?" Ace asked.

Victoria sat up, hands folding on the desk. "No. I'm self-taught in mixing my own makeup, but I've always followed the Good Manufacturing Practice Guidelines to the letter."

"The what?" Ace asked.

"The GMP. It's the Food and Drug Administration's regulations. They don't specify that you need a chemist's license to create makeup. But to be on the safe side, as soon as I got the loan for my own company last year, I hired a cosmetic chemist as a consultant. She's become a full-time employee since we moved into this building in December. And I'm interviewing for a whole research and development team once I get the contract for Boxed & Beautiful."

"Did Daisy Greenbent apply for one of those positions?" Hart asked.

Victoria shook her head. "I was going to hire a team of makeup artists to do some marketing and promotion work, but I ditched the idea. Now I'm trying to get a celeb makeup artist to use my product instead. I had a prominent vlogger all set to do it but, unfortunately, they heard about this whole mess and want to postpone our collaboration." She leaned back in her chair, holding her hands together in her lap.

I glanced sideways at Ace. He only ever used micro-expressions—hard to read when interviewing suspects, but I could tell by the downbeat corner of his lips that her insensitive tone wasn't making the best impression. Officer Hart wore a straightforward frown.

I wanted to tell them to look at Victoria's twisting hands. Then they'd see her all-business attitude was just a mask. She was a ball of nerves in front of them. And she wasn't just thinking about herself. She'd been affected by Mrs. LeBeau's death, deeply. But how could I explain that? My jaw tightened. I wished Victoria would stop bottling her emotions tighter than the seals on the Victress perfumes.

Then I realized how I could help—"Victoria, when did your shipment to Coraline's ship out?"

"Two weeks ago, Friday the tenth." Victoria's eyes widened. Her shoulders finally relaxed. "I did leave early, around 5:00 p.m."

I smiled. "She was with me. We went shopping for presents for our friend's birthday and then out to dinner." I didn't explain that Victoria was helping me pick out Ace's birthday present, but sharp as he was, his brow lifted at the mention. It was subtle and I would have missed it if I hadn't given myself away by glancing in his direction.

I expected Ace and Hart to accept the alibi with no further questioning, but they seemed determined not to drop the inquiry.

Hart asked, "What time did the dinner end?"

Victoria looked at me. "Uh, I don't know. It was early. Six thirty maybe? It was definitely after—oh no, it wasn't." She squeezed her eyes closed and put a hand on her temple. "Noah worked overtime to make up for spending the day at a commercial shoot." Looking at Hart, she added, 'You'll have to ask him when he saw this woman."

I could have guessed Noah was an actor. He had a made-for-TV smile and the air of confidence only seen in someone willing to starve for attention. But I was more interested in Hart's reaction at the moment.

He opened the door. In a curt tone, he said, "We'll do that. Thank you, Miss Jelant. Oh, uh, I should mention we received a warrant to conduct a search of the premises."

"A warrant? But you said it could've just been an allergy." Victoria put a hand to her temple wearily. "The family is already threatening a lawsuit for wrongful death."

"We haven't ruled out homicide, and some new evidence came to light." He glanced at Ace.

I couldn't believe it. Had Ace told him about Sally LeBeau's last words? Even if he had, Hart couldn't have gotten a warrant in ten minutes. Except that he could have—given the proximity of the courthouse to Victress.

Victoria glanced at me with an unreadable expression. She opened the bottom desk drawer and took out her purse. Then she stood near me.

"Do what you have to, Officers. I think I'll go out for some fresh air until you're done." She took my arm and started leading me out.

Hart stood in front of us. "Sorry, Miss Jelant. We'll need to check your bag as well."

Victoria hesitated. Slowly, she slid the strap off and gave up the oversized purse to Hart's care. He gingerly snapped open the button and rifled through the items. It wasn't entirely surprising when he pulled out a couple perfume samples.

Victoria's worried expression bothered me more. She said, "I know that looks, bad but…"

I wrapped an arm around Victoria's shoulder protectively. "She's in the habit of carrying samples. You won't find any poison in that one, I can promise you that."

"We'll just see about that," Hart said.

Chapter 7
Drop Dead Gorgeous

It was 6:00 p.m. on the dot when I received that phone call from Cosima Shine. I finished applying my red lipstick, pressing my lips together to even out the tone, and snatched my cell phone before the third ring.

"Hi, Cosima," I said. "Good to hear from you."

"You're not going to think that in a minute." She sounded annoyed.

"Why's that?" I slipped into my red heels and headed downstairs.

"Because Helen is already in Diamond Springs, so you can expect a visit from her today. She'll be using whatever tactics she can to get you in on the Aria Designs resort show."

"Aria Designs? As in—"

"As in Kent Aria. That's right. She's personally invested in this one. I wouldn't be surprised if she tries to drag you back into your contract."

I nearly stumbled on a step. Personally invested was an understatement. Helen Tegan hadn't just discovered me as a teen for her modeling agency, she'd tried to set me up with her stepson, Kent. In fact, Kent's Adonis-like face had been the one to come to mind upon seeing Noah yesterday. When dating didn't work out for us, Helen kept booking us for the same shows and making our travel arrangements together.

But Kent's modeling career had been shorter than mine. He wasn't serious about modeling, dating, or anything else. I think sometimes Helen's goal was more about me being a good influence on him.

In a way, I was happy to hear he was running his own fashion show. I'd seen some of his designs in that black sketchbook and always hoped his talent for fashion would outweigh his predilection for partying.

Cosima continued, "I know Kent didn't make the best impression, but he has turned a corner, Kait. I'm not saying I agree with Helen pushing you two together personally, but professionally I think you'd be a good fit for his show. We need a cool head around here."

"He's being temperamental, isn't he?"

Head Over Heels

"The temperament of genius. The designs really are extraordinary. But, yes, three models threatened to quit. We already lost our hair and makeup teams. I don't think this show will go through without you."

"So, you're calling to warn me about Helen, or to convince me to come back with her?"

"All right, I won't push you. I did call to warn you, but I thought you might want to hear what's going on before you see her. I've got to go. Just think about what I said, okay?"

"Okay," I hung up the phone found my purse on the counter in the foyer when the doorbell rang.

I checked my watch, a silver, rhinestone-studded Swarovski band. A half hour awaited me before dinner, and my date was supposed to meet me at the restaurant, unless Scarlett had changed the plan.

Last chance. I gave myself the once-over in the mirror. I looked ready, but I didn't feel it. I wasn't sure I should be going out while Victoria was waiting to hear about the results of the testing on the perfume bottle. She insisted she was fine, and Ava had stepped in to take her out to dinner. So, I had no excuses to put off what could either be a huge disappointment or the beginning of a life-changing romance.

I opened the door—and froze. Ace did the same, blinking as if seeing me for the first time. He was dressed in the same suit he was wearing this morning, but he'd shaved his five o'clock shadow and added the jacket he rarely ever wore, which emphasized his broad shoulders.

"It's you?" I asked.

He ran a hand through his hair. "I-I'm sorry to interrupt your plans. You have a date?"

My shoulders fell. If he didn't know about my blind date, Ace certainly couldn't be him. I forced a smile. "Just a blind date a friend set up for me—nothing serious." I felt my stomach twinge against my words.

Nothing serious? Why was I explaining my date to him? Why did he look interested? I pushed a blonde strand behind my ear, hoping to hide the blush I could feel rising to my cheeks. Quickly changing the subject, I said, "What's going on?"

The hint of amusement on Ace's face faded, piquing my interest. "I know you're still angry with me from this morning."

I shook my head. "You said you didn't tell Hart and I believe you. I'm not angry."

He ran a hand through his thick brown hair. "You might be after I tell you this: Victoria has been arrested."

Head Over Heels

So many questions flashed through my mind, such as *what? when?* and—"Why? Did the police find poison in the perfume?"

"All the perfume in the store came back negative. The one in Victoria's purse was laced with arsenic. Kait, it doesn't look good."

"She's obviously being framed," I said, leaving Ace at the door as I switched into my lavender heels. It made it easy that I kept all my going-out shoes in the downstairs walk-in closet under the stairs. I grabbed my matching trench coat and wrapped it around me. Then, I walked out into the cold, heading straight to Ace's car.

I felt his eyes following me as he caught up. Ace's gait surpassed me to the passenger door, which he opened for me. I briefly pictured us driving to a restaurant instead of a police station. Suddenly, I didn't regret missing the blind date.

The thought prompted me to take out my phone and message Scarlett. She'd have to understand, or, apparently, she already did. She must have texted while I was still on the phone with Cosima, because I found a message from her, stating simply: *Forget dinner. You'll meet at Ace's birthday celebration.*

I caught myself in the middle of a horrified jaw-drop. I couldn't think of a worse place to meet someone than at the home of the man I had feelings for—feelings I probably shouldn't have, considering he was my boss.

My phone started buzzing. I slipped inside the car and answered as Ace walked around to his side and started the vehicle.

"Ava? Wait, slow down."

She repeated the words I hadn't heard properly the first time. "I'm bailing Victoria out right now and taking her home, but she wants you to, oh, okay, fine."

"Kait?" Victoria came on the line.

"I'm here. Are you okay?"

"Yeah, fine," Victoria said, sounding anything but that. "Look, I wouldn't ask you to cancel your date, but I'm being framed here."

"I know. We're going to find out who is setting you up."

"I think I already know. I just didn't want to admit it. I'm sure you noticed I was aware of the perfume bottle in my purse."

I watched Ace from the corner of my eye. He hadn't started the car and was looking at me. I spoke cautiously, "Yes."

"I swear the first time I noticed it was in there was at Sycamore's. Someone slipped it into my purse and the only people who would've had access to it were Noah and

Tara. You know my chemist, Tara. I'm sure you met her once."

I vaguely recalled an Asian-American woman around Victoria's age who looked younger than me with a short bob and a casual wardrobe.

"I remember. Didn't she call in sick today?"

"Yes, and she's been pretty distant with me lately."

"Interesting. Any idea why?" I asked, putting it on speaker for Ace to listen in.

"Not until today. She left me a message on my phone saying she knew that I was poisoning the perfumes and that she won't work for a murderess."

"She thinks you're guilty?" I couldn't believe it.

"I think she's covering for herself. She had access to everything. She knew where I kept my purse. And, she has a history. She had an incident in college where a classmate threatened to sue when a skin cream she made gave her a rash. When I hired her, I believed her when she said that was a false accusation, especially after my experience with Sally LeBeau. But what if it wasn't?"

"But why would she target Sally LeBeau?"

"Maybe she didn't. But if she made a mistake again—something to make my products defective—she might want to cover that up."

"By putting poison in the make up? That seems extreme," I said.

Victoria thought about that for a moment. "I don't know. She's been acting strangely for a while—distant, cold. Maybe she *is* extreme—you know, *disturbed*. Could you just check her out?"

I looked at Ace with questioning eyes. He took out his notebook and nodded. "Okay. Give us the address," I said.

"It's 2555 West Cavalier Street," Victoria replied.

"We're on it. Just hang tight."

"Not sure I can. I'll be too busy doing damage control. LeBeau's family tipped off a ton of reporters—I had to dodge them coming out of the jail. With this negative coverage, all my deals are falling through. Turns out no one wants to do business with a company whose products have killed a person. But I'll turn this around. I just have to figure out how to spin the publicity."

"I'm sure you will," I said, and I meant it. If anyone could find the advantage in such a disadvantageous situation, it was Victoria.

Hanging up the phone, I watched Ace start the car.

"Tara sounds like a pretty convincing suspect, doesn't she?" I asked.

Ace took a deep breath. "If Tara made some kind of mistake with the perfume, sure. It's possible."

Head Over Heels

"You don't believe it?"

"I believe facts. A fact we confirmed at Victress is that Victoria controls the ingredients, checks the product, and personally oversees shipments. If the product was defective, how could she not notice?"

"She's not a chemist like Tara."

"A chemist who should know how to mix makeup."

I felt heat rising in my cheeks. My face must have been red when Ace looked at me, because he added quickly, "I'm not saying I don't believe Victoria. I'm just reserving my judgment until we talk to Tara. We can agree on that, can't we?"

Part of me knew he was right. But couldn't he just trust that I knew Victoria couldn't murder anyone? I didn't want to argue, so I changed the subject instead.

I noticed Ace hadn't programmed the address into the GPS. I didn't see where one was located in his car. So, I looked around the dashboard.

"Do you not have a GPS in your car, or do you know the way?"

"I'm familiar with the neighborhood," he said. "And no, not every car has fancy built-in systems."

I set my phone in a broken cupholder between us, realizing I'd forgotten my purse. I wasn't going to ask him to go back for it, not after an argument and not when we were so close to getting Victoria off the hook.

"I sign your invoices, you know. You can afford a better car than this," I said, wishing we'd taken my Bentley. Looking at his suit, I added, "At least the clothes are an improvement over your usual three alternating suits."

He touched his jacket collar and shrugged. "I mix and match sometimes."

"If you weren't *you*, you'd never get away with it," I said, thinking about how my anger toward him was still somehow tempered by how I felt about him—how I couldn't help but feel.

He furrowed his brow, seemingly befuddled. "What does that mean?"

I scrambled for an answer. "You know, since you're a renowned detective, no one pays attention to your wardrobe."

Thankfully, we reached the house by the end of my sentence. It sat a street away from the lake for which Diamond Springs was named. I could see the crystal-clear water against the dimming sunlight in the distance. Homes here were newer cookie-cutters that were not without appeal, but had less personality than the old estates in my area.

Head Over Heels

Ever the gentleman, Ace opened the passenger door and I stepped out into the spring night, realizing I was overdressed for an interrogation. Ace led the way to the front door and rang the bell. We heard a yipping followed by "down girl," then a slow creak as the door opened. Tara held her tan sweater close around her neck and kept the door chain in place.

"Miss Yan?" Ace said.

"Yes?"

Taking out his notebook, Ace said, "I'm P.I. Aeson East, and this is my associate, Kaitlynn Sasse. We'd like to ask you a few questions about the death of Sally LeBeau. Do you mind if we—"

"Yes, I mind. I already told the police I've been out sick the last few days. I don't know anything about Mrs. LeBeau."

"The bottle would've been shipped out a couple weeks ago. You were involved in that shipment," I said.

"Those products were not poisoned," came the defensive reply.

"The perfume tester was," I said.

"Like I told the police, those were all part of the same batch, but Victoria packaged the testers herself. She always checks the shipments personally."

I grimaced. That was nearly verbatim with what Noah had said except for one detail. "Did you return to Victress late in the evening on Monday of last week?"

Tara blinked. "What? No, why."

"There was a woman in a burgundy coat seen in the stockroom room the night before the shipment to Coraline's," I said.

"It must've been Victoria," Tara said.

"She has an alibi," I said, ignoring the side-eyed glance from Ace.

He didn't contradict me. Instead, he said, "Is there anyone else you know who may have had access to the Victress office?"

Tara clamped her jaw tight. I could see doubt in her darting eyes, but the crisis of conscience passed. "I don't know," she said. Then she started to close the door.

I pushed past Ace. "We know about the incident in your past, Miss Yan. You've been accused of poisoning a cosmetic product before."

Tara stopped. She glared through the screen. "That was a misunderstanding. Char and I were arguing at the time, but she withdrew the complaint."

"Char?" Ace asked.

"The girl who accused me. She was my roommate in college. She can vouch for me."

Head Over Heels

"Do you have her contact information?" Ace asked.

Tara's eyes shifted to her left. "She's my neighbor. The house on the corner with the rosebushes is hers."

"Your college roommate became your neighbor?" Ace asked.

Perhaps it was the word neighbor that prompted an old woman's voice to call out, "Tara? Why are you standing at the door like that? If you have visitors, let them in."

Tara opened the door wide enough for Ace and me to enter. A woman with smooth skin and gray hair introduced herself as Tara's mother. She offered to make us tea and disappeared into the kitchen.

Tara sat reluctantly on a sofa chair while Ace and I took the couch in the sitting room. Teacups and decorative plates gave the place a homey feel, but Tara's expression was cold as she explained.

"My neighbor became my college roommate. We went to high school together. I moved back here two years ago to help my mom take care of my father. He passed away just a few months ago. Char just came back last month. She bought the old house her parents used to own before they moved to the city."

I hadn't gone to high school in Diamond Springs, but I had visited her grandparents enough summers to know that the town had only one high school. When I'd met Victoria, I was still a tween, but she had already graduated and was working in Ava's parents' shoe store and experimenting with makeup. She gave plenty of free makeovers and sample products to anyone who would give her feedback, and we thought she was the coolest girl ever.

Victoria had gone from leading roles in her high school drama classes to senior class president to owning a rapidly growing cosmetics business. If Tara had gone to school in town, the chances were that she would have at least heard of Victoria Jelant.

"Did you and Victoria know each other from high school as well?" I asked.

"I knew *of* Victoria, everyone did, but no, Char and I were two grades below her. I don't think she'd remember us."

There was a bitterness in her tone that Ace and I both caught.

"Miss Yan, I hope you'll forgive the question, but it doesn't sound like you like your boss very much," Ace noted.

Tara sighed. "Look, I don't have a problem with her. She's been fine as a boss. But do I trust her? No. If you want to know how she really is, she's the type of person who would give a homemade chocolate bar with almonds in it to a person with nut allergies just so they would withdraw in an audition for a play."

"She wouldn't do that." I sat straight on the edge of my chair, nearly leaping out of it.

"She did this to you?" Ace asked.

"Not me. Char. She had to go to the hospital. I'd forgotten all about it until Char reminded me. She didn't want to accuse Victoria at the time—she looked up to her so much, but when Char found out I work for her, she told me. So, you can see why after this mess, I just can't work for someone like that."

"Victoria isn't 'someone like that.' She's competitive, but not without scruples. She'd never have deliberately hurt your friend," I said.

"Just like she didn't hurt Sally LeBeau? I really want to believe that, but I'm sorry, I believe my friend." Tara stood as her mother walked into the room with a tray of tea and sugar cookies. "Sorry, Mom, they were just leaving."

Ace and I stood. I almost felt bad for Tara. This Char person was clearly manipulating her. I just didn't know why. I thanked Mrs. Yan and headed to the door.

"One more thing," Ace said before they reached the threshold. "Did your friend Char ever visit Victress Cosmetics?"

"No, um, yeah, maybe she picked me up once or twice. She works at the mall, so sometimes we carpool."

"Did you carpool last Monday?" I asked.

Tara crossed her arms, realization washing over her features. "No."

Ace smiled. "Thank you for your time, Miss Yan."

As we closed the door, I said, "I believe her. I don't think she did it, but I do think Char is a good suspect."

Ace nodded. "We can question her tomorrow. Um, since you didn't have any dinner, are you hungry?"

"Yes." I smiled.

Scarlett might kill me for canceling, but I didn't care, as long as Ace was offering.

"Great," he said. "We can pick something up on the way."

"The way where?" My eyes narrowed, unsure what to expect, but, knowing Ace, he meant something work-related.

"I've closed out two of our other cases, but we still have the third to work."

I kept my tone even. "Which one?"

Head Over Heels

He leaned on the open door, looking down at me as I sat inside. "The cheating husband case. I thought we'd do a little spying tonight."

I fake-smiled. My plans for the evening still involved a date at a fancy restaurant. Only instead of being on a date, I've be watching one through a lens.

Chapter 8

Under Her Skin

In the morning, while Ace finished our other cases and confirmed the information Tara gave us, I returned to the scene of the crime. I hadn't dismissed Daisy as a suspect the way Ace had done. The second I'd heard she'd been released from the hospital, I knew I had to see her.

After an unsuccessful trip to her home, I learned from a man who looked as ill as Daisy had been that she had returned to work today. The store was still closed to the public, though, with just a few staff helping set up for the re-opening. I supposed she thought she could handle a day without customers. When I arrived at the Blue Diamond, Daisy was not working but seated at the tiny coffee stand and bakery outside Coraline's, Café & Cupcakes.

Head Over Heels

Daisy looked pale, like a woman who might have needed to stay in the hospital rather than be out and about working. Her smiled faltered as I approached. She kept her eyes downcast, focusing on her tea as if meditating.

"Daisy? I'm Kait, I was here when...the incident happened."

She glanced up and back at the table. Nodding, she said, "I remember. You're the friend who was with Victoria Jelant."

"I'm also an investigator trying to help with the case. Do you mind if I ask you a few questions?"

She held a hand out toward the empty chair across from her. "I'd like to help. I've been worried people might think I poisoned Mrs. LeBeau. Well, I mean, I did spray the perfume, but I didn't poison it."

I tried a reassuring smile as she swiped a piece of hair out of her teary eyes. Daisy opened her lab coat and reached into a pocket tucked on the inside. It was a concealed compartment that held a full-sized wallet stuffed to the brim with receipts and bills, and a tissue, which she took out. The inner pocket must be deceptively big. I wasn't sure why that was important, but I mentally filed it for later.

"I'm glad you're feeling better," I said. "It's a good thing you didn't inhale too much of the perfume."

"I didn't inhale it. Some of it got on my hands. The top of the container leaked a little. It was on my fingers long enough that I guess it made me sick. The doctors figured it out pretty quickly. Arsenic and perfumes have a history."

"Do they?" I asked.

Daisy leaned forward. "Did you ever read Femme Fatale? I just started reading the book on Lottie's recommendation and it talks about the exact type of poisoning. A woman named Giulia Tofana used arsenic in a perfume—she called it Aqua Tofana. It made the perfect weapon for women to off their husbands in the 17th century. No one suspected the perfume. It's fascinating, but I never expected to happen in my lifetime."

"That is fascinating," I agreed. "Lottie recommended the book?"

"Yes, she read it online. The writer was a blogger originally. She put her posts together to make the book."

I mulled that over. Lottie knew about Aqua Tofana, she was behind the counter when Daisy dropped the perfume, and she wore the same lab coat as Daisy—one that was large enough to hide a perfume bottle inside and then stash somewhere later, like in Victoria's purse.

"Daisy, Lottie said you signed the delivery slip. Is that normal for you?"

"No. Lottie was busy and I was working overtime, so she asked me to sign it."

I nodded. That lined up with what Lottie had said. "Was there anything unusual in the shipment?"

"No. Well, I thought I had unpacked the testers and set them out, but yesterday morning I noticed that I'd put out a regular bottle of perfume instead of the tester. I don't know how I made that mistake. Lottie was pretty mad."

"Why were you so adamant about spraying Mrs. LeBeau with the perfume?"

Daisy glanced around. "I know it looks suspicious, but I was just following orders. Lottie knew that Mrs. LeBeau was coming in and she said that Ella wanted to personally impress LeBeau with Victress's product, so I absolutely had to get her to try the perfume—at the very least. She insisted. That's why I sprayed it."

"You told the police this?"

"Yes."

I sat in silence, thinking. The police must have taken it as tracing it back to Victoria. Hart might say that she's friends with Ella and manipulated both Ella and Lottie and the whole situation.

Daisy filled in my silence. "I'm sorry your friend was accused. She seems nice. I really wanted to work for her."

I leaned forward. "What about your current boss? Are you happy at the Blue Diamond?"

She tried for a smile. In an almost squeaky voice, she said, "I don't want to say a bad word about Ella, but…"

"Oh, no. I should've said Coraline's, not the mall, sorry. I meant Lottie," I corrected.

I didn't dispute the suspicion Daisy cast on Ella, but I didn't see her as a murder suspect. Ella would never kill anyone. She'd have no way of belittling them beyond the grave.

Though, she did have devilish hearing, considering she appeared before us seconds after speaking of her. Ella homed in on Daisy. She and her crony, a.k.a. a security guard, stood beside Daisy's chair.

"Miss Greenbent, an officer just came to my office with a warrant for your locker, so, I have to ask you to go with him and open it for the officers."

Daisy stood and began to walk away. Ella stayed behind. Crossing her arms, she looked at me point blank. I raised my eyebrows and waited for a snarky comment to sneak out her lips.

Head Over Heels

"Advice from a friend: don't question people on your own. Daisy is a regular here. I wouldn't be surprised if she had a way of poisoning your drink."

My brows lifted even higher. I realized now what it was in Ella that had remained true all these years: she'd always had a way of learning people's secrets.

"You really do pay attention to people, don't you?" I asked.

For a mall so large, the Blue Diamond hosted more workers than any mall manager could know individually. Yet, she knew each person Ace and I had questioned well enough that I wondered if she did somehow keep track of each employee.

"I pay attention when they're associated with my friends."

I leaned back and looked up at her. "You do consider Victoria a friend, don't you?"

I asked the question sarcastically...and regretted it. There was something in Ella's eyes I hadn't noticed before. Pain. She breathed in sharply.

"I'm just trying to make sure this mall doesn't see another homicide on my watch," she said. Then she turned.

"Wait," I said. I hesitated. I wasn't going to apologize, mostly because she wouldn't have accepted it if I did. She tended to see apologies as a sign of weakness. But I knew she'd interpret my next words as a sort of reconciliation.

"I could use your help. What do you know about the store manager, Lottie Hambledon?"

Ella squinted as if studying my intent. Then, she sat where Daisy had been seated a moment ago. Her tone lacked its normal disdain.

"Not much. She applied here a year ago for a mall cart with cosmetics products, but Victoria was already established and her products were too similar, so I turned her down. She was with a branch of Coraline's in the city and transferred here when this branch opened."

"Have you noticed anything suspicious about her?"

"Like what?"

I shrugged. "Odd behavior, customer complaints, things like that."

Ella shook her head. "Not that I know of offhand, but I can check Charlotte's file and get back to you."

"Thanks," I said, trying to keep the surprise out of my voice. I hadn't thought of Ella as a suspect, despite our mutual dislike. But this, being nice to me, that I found deeply suspicious.

I hadn't changed my mind about her not being involved in the murder. But Ella had given me enough information for me to change my mind about her. And, more importantly, I'd changed my mind about my prime suspect. It wasn't Daisy anymore.

It was Charlotte "Lottie" Hambledon.

Chapter 9

All Made Up

Ace leaned back in the executive chair in his office, spinning a pencil between his fingers casually. He looked up and smiled when I walked in. I wasn't surprised to see him in the office on a Sunday, though I wasn't expecting to see him looking happy. I welcomed the change in his demeanor but gave him a questioning look.

He dropped the pencil onto the desk, greeting me with the words: "You were right."

I crossed my arms. "Words every woman wants to hear. What precisely are you admitting I was right about?"

He handed me a file. "I had second thoughts when I heard Victoria's prints were on the bottle, but not Daisy's. So, I checked the other bottles. The prints are similar on all of them. She touched the tips of each one, as if counting off on them."

"The way a person would if they were checking a shipment?" I asked.

Ace nodded. "Some of the bottles included Tara's prints, some Noah's, but all of them had Victoria's in common. If the woman Noah saw in the stockroom was wearing gloves—"

"The culprit's prints wouldn't be on the bottle," I finished his thought.

I'd been so focused on suspects, I hadn't followed up on the fingerprints.

"I think you're right about someone framing Victoria," Ace said.

I could've kissed him.

I sat across from him in the chair usually reserved for clients, saying, "I'm glad you came around. While you're running lab reports, you might check the pockets of the Coraline lab coats. There's a secret pocket that would be ideal for sneaking out a product like one of the Victress perfumes. According to Daisy, the perfume bottle was leaky. If a Coraline employee tried to sneak the bottle out of the store, it might've left a trace in the pocket."

"Noted. Scarlett told me you had moved on to Daisy as a suspect. I think Daisy Greenbent is our gal."

I winced. "Actually, I don't think Daisy is responsible."

Ace sat forward, the old chair squeaking as he put his hands on the desk. "Who's your suspect now?"

"Lottie Hambledon. Or Char. Remember, from our interview with Tara. She said her friend 'Char' had had a problem with Victoria, and today Ella called 'Lottie' Charlotte. Both are nicknames for the same person."

"Well, you are right about that. Charlotte Hambledon is Tara's neighbor on Cavalier Street."

I gave him a satisfied smile. He shook his head and smiled back. Now that Ace was leaning away from Victoria as a suspect, we could relax around each other. I'd missed that.

"I think we've got our killer. Lottie had a motive, means, and opportunity."

"You'll have to explain to me," Ace said.

I ticked imaginary boxes with my finger. "Motive: she applied for a cosmetic cart at the Blue Diamond and they denied her since Victoria's cart was already there. Means: she went to Victress all the time to pick up her friend, Tara. Opportunity: Coraline's has a list of shipments and estimated arrival times, and she has a friend who works there, so she could've figured out when Victress would be shipping its products."

Ace's lips dipped like they always did when he was about to disagree with me. I crossed my arms and cocked my head, like I did when I was ready to prove him wrong.

"I agree, that could be a motive. But I don't like to jump to conclusions. Daisy's motivation was just as strong. She had access to the perfume, a means of hiding it, she knew her target, and she had a motive."

"What motive?" I asked.

"Before she retired and became a mystery shopper, Sally LeBeau worked as a bank manager. She was known for how often she denied loans. She foreclosed on Daisy's parents' business when her father became ill. They've been struggling financially ever since."

My lips pressed tight. Now I understood what Daisy had meant about needing the money. But LeBeau's death wouldn't help her situation. And Scarlett was right about her not seeming to be the type to murder someone— especially for revenge.

I refocused on Charlotte. "We were planning to talk to 'Char' anyway, right? Why don't we at least question her again?"

"It's always a good idea to gather more facts," Ace agreed.

"She's at Coraline's and the store is closed."

Astoria Wright

"All right. We can catch her tomorrow before she goes to work."

I grinned. I would definitely catch Charlotte Hambledon tomorrow.

Chapter 10
Smoke and Mirrors

I was well-prepared to confront Lottie in the morning. I was much less prepared to see Helen Teagan standing on the other side of the door as I stepped out to start my day. She did not look well. Thinner, paler, and much more haggard than I remembered her, Helen opened her arms for a hug.

"Kait, surprised to see me?" She pulled me into a hug, which I reciprocated hesitantly.

"I did have a little heads up," I said as we pulled away.

"That Cosima. She's a spoilsport ruining my surprise. Can I come in? I could use a strong cup of coffee."

"Actually, I was just on my way—"

Helen entered the doorway before I could finish the sentence.

"Oh, it's just as I remembered. You even kept your grandmother's furniture!"

"Helen, I know you've come to ask my help, but," I stopped. The bags below her eyes showed through her makeup. I frowned. I couldn't just turn her away after she'd made such a long drive up here. "Why don't you come into the kitchen and I'll get you that coffee you wanted."

Relief flooded Helen's face. She followed me past the foyer, beyond the stairs, and into the kitchen, where she sat at the table. Fidgeting with the placemat, she stared out the sliding doors into the garden. Everything bloomed this time of year, but Helen's smile had faded. It took only a minute to pour two cups from the still-warm coffee machine and fill a creamer. I brought the drinks over and sat across from Helen.

She spoke tiredly as she poured the cream into her coffee. "I suppose Cosima told you why I wanted to see you."

"Yes. Kent's first show as a designer is exciting. You must be proud."

She smiled. "I am, so proud. His designs are incredible, and I'm not just saying that as his stepmother."

"I know. I remember his sketches."

Head Over Heels

Helen patted my hand. "You were always so good to him. I know it didn't work out between you, and I can't blame you, not one bit. But he has pulled his life together. He still has a..."

"An artist's temperament?" I offered.

She chuckled. "That's right. It's perfect or not at all. It's always been that way in his life, his art, even his performances. 'Nothing and no one is ever good enough' he says—not even him. You were the only one he thought came close."

I felt my cheeks reddening. I had rejected Kent, but I hadn't thought he was terrible. He wasn't even close to the worst date I'd ever had. I wondered how he'd related our breakup to her. Helen was smart enough to figure out why things were so short-lived between us, given Kent's emotional instability. She was also self-deceiving enough to ignore anything wrong in Kent, his relationships, or his life. Apparently, she could see it now.

"I heard you had some people quit."

"Models, makeup artists, runners; the wardrobe assistants are hanging by a thread—no pun—but I've managed to keep enough of them. I need help, Kait. You were always a problem solver. You know, because of you, there have been some changes at the agency." My eyes had drifted away from Helen as she spoke. I had heard that the agent who had goaded a model into an eating disorder and then cut her from the agency had been fired. But I still hadn't saved my model-friend from herself.

"I can't persuade you to come back, can I? Not to the agency, but just for the show?" Helen asked.

I sipped the coffee and set it down slowly. I had met good people in the industry over the years. There were makeup artists and others whom I knew would respond to a call for help.

"I know you want Kent's show to succeed. I want that, too. I could call some of my contacts and see who's free to help. But, I'm sorry, that's all I can do."

Helen drank her coffee like the last drops of a wine cooler. "I'm a wreck, Kait." She laughed. "It's Kent's show and *I'm* a wreck."

I gave a sympathetic wince. Kent had that mind-wrecking effect on people. It took a strong person to not feel bothered by critical eyes like Kent's. That gave me an idea.

"Say, Helen, I noticed you're not looking like your usual self." I walked over to my purse in the foyer and shuffled through the items in it as I walked back. "Why don't you get some rest in the guest room and when you're up to it, try a little pick-me-up like this." I handed her the coupon from Coraline's.

Head Over Heels

"A free makeover?" She handed it back. "I'd go to a spa if I had the time. Thanks for the reminder about my looks, by the way."

I pushed the coupon back and gave a good-natured laugh. "You're beautiful, but you're also looking for a new makeup team, right? Well, there's a brand at Coraline's I think you should try and a talented makeup artist who might just agree to do a show with you. Just ask for Daisy and tell her I sent you."

Helen perked up. "Really? Well, I might just do that then. Thank you, Kait." She downed the rest of her coffee, leaving me wondering how her throat wasn't burning. Then, Helen headed back out the door.

She called behind her, "I'll just take my things to the guest room. You go ahead where you were going, dear. Don't mind me!"

I didn't have the time to mind anything. Rushing out, I took my car to meet Ace in Lottie's neighborhood. My built-in GPS brought me through the town to a corner home on Rose and Cavalier Streets. Rosebushes and hanging plants swayed in the wind on a dilapidated porch. I wrapped the belt on my trench coat and looked down the road for Ace's Hyundai.

"Looking for me?" Ace's voice came out of nowhere.

I clutched my heart. "Where did you come from?" I asked, not seeing his Hyundai in the road.

He chuckled. "I live around the corner." He pointed to the sign that read *Cavalier Street.*

My cheeks reddened. I could see now why my joke about the street name hadn't gone over well with Ace. It was his neighborhood.

I laughed as we walked up the driveway. "I'm glad it was just you and not some crazed lunatic. This house is like a bad horror movie."

"Don't breathe a sigh of relief just yet." Ace ran up the porch. Smoke streamed out of the windows.

The house was on fire.

Chapter 11

Concealer

Ace crashed through the door. I followed him into the kitchen where a pan was burning on the stove. Lottie lay sprawled on the floor. Ace scooped her up, shouting, "Kait, get out, now!"

I opened a cupboard, then another.

"What are you doing?"

I ignored Ace. Despite the smoke, the fire hadn't gone past the stove. I found a cooking sheet and slapped it on top of the pan. The fire subsided, but the smoke didn't. I began to cough. The world took on the look of a charcoal sketch.

A strong arm wrapped around my torso. The scent of Ace's sea breeze cologne revived me as he held me to his chest. Within seconds, we breached the door. Ace set me down so that my heels sank into soft grass. He didn't let go until my coughing stopped and my lungs filled with fresh air. One hand still on my back, Ace brushed the hair out of my face in a gentle stroke.

"Are you all right?" he asked.

I nodded. I almost regretted the admission that I was fine. His fingers slid away from me.

Lottie moaned where she lay in the grass. Ace walked to her side. With his cell phone in hand, he dialed 911. Lottie's hand shot out to Ace's wrist.

"What are you doing?" she said. Then she launched into a coughing fit.

"Take it easy," Ace consoled her. "The fire's out, but you've inhaled a lot of smoke. I'm calling for an ambulance."

Lottie pushed back the strands of her frazzled hair. Between coughs, she said, "No, I'm fine."

"You're not," I said.

"No, I—" She put a hand to her forehead, struggling. "The fire's out, right? So everything's fine."

Ace and I exchanged a glance.

"Tell you what," Ace said, "there's still a lot of smoke in the house. I live right up the road, why don't you take a breather with us a while until we're sure that you're okay."

Head Over Heels

Lottie nodded. With Ace's help, she sat in the back of my car. Ace and I sat in the front. I kept glancing in the rearview to see that Lottie was still sitting upright.

"What happened?" I asked.

"I…I was preparing my lunch and Tara, my neighbor, came over. We were arguing and I told her to leave, then I went back to preparing my breakfast." In the rearview, Lottie was shaking her head. "I don't remember anything after that."

We drove just halfway down the road to a home with a white picket fence and a blue door. I recognized the Hyundai in the driveway, but nothing else about the home was mediocre.

Leaning on Ace, Lottie limped to the door. Ace opened it for us to walk through. Lottie caught sight of herself in a mirror in the foyer.

She ran her fingers through her hair, saying, "Oh, I look awful."

She did, but I didn't think it was polite to point that out. Ace gestured toward the outer hallway.

"You're welcome to use the restroom to wash up."

"Thank you," Lottie replied, making her way down the hall.

I flashed Ace a look. He put a hand out for my arm, then dropped a keyset into my hands. I raised an eyebrow, turning the keychain over. Beside the keys was the letter T, presumably for Tara. I interpreted it differently than I knew Ace would.

"She stole this. It has the keys to Victress Cosmetics. Don't you see, that's how she got in and planted the poison."

Ace crossed his arms and frowned. "Or Tara left them there in a hurry after setting fire to Lottie's home."

I stood with my mouth agape. It wasn't unreasonable. I didn't know what to believe, and I was tired of arguing with Ace. He walked up the steps into the kitchen and grabbed the phone to report the incident to the police.

I took the time to investigate my surroundings. I'd never been to Ace's home before. It was the complete opposite of his untidy workspace at the office. The kitchen and adjacent living room coordinated between blue and white with impeccable taste. Even now, when I could throttle Ace for his blind arrogance about this case, I felt drawn to the décor, relishing the insight into his personality. The foyer dropped down into the kitchen with its all white cabinets and multi-shade blue mosaic tiles. Past the kitchen and up two steps sat a navy-blue sofa. The naval trinkets that completed the room I soon realized were not mere souvenirs.

Head Over Heels

I touched the edge of a shadow box full of awards. "You were in the Navy?"

Ace clicked off the phone and walked toward me. "No, my father and grandfather. I guess I broke the tradition."

"Your heart wasn't in it?"

"Uh, no. It turned out my father's wasn't. He had a whole other family in Connecticut. When my mother found out, she was heartbroken. After that, I made a promise to myself that I'd stay in town, watch out for her and my little sister."

I looked at him with a renewed sense of awe. "You helped keep your family together."

He smiled. "They're strong women. They would've been fine, but I'm glad I could be here. Plus, I found I had a knack for crime investigation. I did well for myself."

"And your mom?"

"She lives in an old-age resort in town. Maisie and I both offered her a place to stay, but she's too independent for it."

"She sounds tough," Lottie said, interrupting our moment.

Ace walked away from me. "You should rest. The police are on their way."

"What, why? It was just a small fire," Lottie protested.

"You fainted after arguing with a neighbor. I think it's best if Officer Hart just hears your story. You said Tara was with you?" Ace asked.

Lottie looked like she might argue, but then she thought better of it. "Yeah. I can't remember things clearly. She was leaving, then I...I don't know what happened. I just woke up on the floor. You don't think she attacked me, do you?"

"Should we think that?" I asked. Something about her tone seemed like she was reaching.

"She came over in a huff. It was something about Victress and the murder case. She was turning accusations on all kinds of people, including me at one point. She was delusional." She sank into a chair by the kitchen island.

Ace offered her a drink of water, which she accepted eagerly. I noticed the rash on her forearm as she lifted the glass, the puffiness of her cheeks as she drank, and how she clutched her side and winced when setting the glass down. Her fall and the shock of the fire might explain all that. But ideas flickered in my brain, re-sparking my suspicion.

By the time Lottie had wiped her chin, there was a knock at the door. Ace let Officer Hart in and he sat with

Lottie on the couch, taking notes of the same story she told us. I pulled Ace away.

In the foyer, I whispered, "I might know why Lottie fainted. It wasn't Tara."

"What, then?" he asked.

"I can't be sure. I have to check it out. Tell Hart to meet me tomorrow at Coraline's re-opening."

"Why?"

"If I'm right, I know exactly who killed Sally LeBeau."

"Can you provide Hart with actual proof?" Ace asked.

I spun on a heel toward the door, saying, "Oh, I can do better than that."

Chapter 12

Eye of the Beholder

Officer Hart was not pleased to meet Ace and me inside Coraline's department store on their new grand opening. He and Jones navigated the crowds with a grimace on his face. He shook his head when he bumped into a shopper five feet from me. The woman gave him a devil-eye as he apologized.

"You sure know how to pick the worst days to meet at a mall, Miss Sasse," he said when he reached us.

I winced, recalling last year's Black Friday mishap. "Sorry, but I thought it would be best to close this out here and now."

"So, who are we here to arrest this time?" Jones clutched the handcuffs fastened to his belt.

My hand shot out to hover over his. "I can't tell you that. Not yet. What I need is for you put those away and take a look at the blond man with the exceptional cheekbones over there."

Ace tilted his head sideways at the mention of the cheekbones, but I stood by my description. Hart recognized Noah from his visit to Victress. He took a step forward. Ace put an arm on his shoulder.

"Just watch. Don't interfere—not yet," he said.

Noah walked up to Lottie and leaned over the counter. Lottie's eyes widened and she looked at him sternly. Despite glaring daggers, she nodded and left her post. She stopped the nearest saleswoman and gave some instruction, to which the woman nodded. Then she headed through the store.

Hart and Jones began to follow.

"Wait," I said, "I know where they're going. There's another way in."

I walked out of Coraline's and into a side door off the mall. A staff-only hallway took us to a shipping area. Ella appeared in the hall a few feet in.

"This way. She's inside." Ella waved us through.

'Inside' meant Coraline's stockroom, specifically the row of cosmetics products near the entrance opposite us. Through the boxes, Lottie's voice was muffled but distinct enough to make out the words.

"What is it exactly you think you saw?" she asked.

"You in the Victress stockroom," Noah answered.

"That's preposterous."

"You could try to deny it, but I can prove it was you."

"Oh really? How?" I could see through the sporting goods boxes now. Lottie crossed her arms, smirking skeptically.

"Surveillance cameras," Noah said.

"There were no—" Lottie's smile disappeared. Her arms fell to her hips.

It was hard to tell if she realized she was being caught in a lie or that she was being blackmailed. I guessed the latter.

Her eyes narrowed. Her scowl portrayed a murderous rage, but her voice was calm when she asked, "How much do you want?"

Noah kept calm. "I think that info is worth at least ten grand. Don't you?"

"Is that all? Not a problem."

Suddenly, the noise shifted, as if they we're moving around in the room.

I glanced at Ace and Hart. The lead officer pointed to his deputy, then down the row. Jones took the hint, walking briskly but silently down the aisle. Hart and Ace walked the other way. Ella and I tiptoed along with the voices.

Head Over Heels

"Maybe I should ask for more," Noah joked. His acting skills deserved an Oscar. I was beginning to worry they might get him killed instead. He and Lottie stopped a few paces away. Ace, Ella, and I moved along with them, as hushed as possible. Officers Hart and Jones headed in opposite directions down the aisle. Hopefully, they'd corner her before she could make any move against Noah.

With the adrenaline pumping from my head to my heels, I jumped back when Ella tapped my shoulder. She held both hands up in a "calm down" gesture, then pointed. I followed her direction and squinted between the boxes.

I didn't see her at first, but then, standing between the packages on the aisle opposite of us, was a figure. Concentrating, I made out who was lurking in the shadows.

"What's Victoria doing here?" I mouthed.

"I let her in," Ella whispered. "I didn't think she'd get so close, though."

Spotting me, Victoria put a hand up. I shook my head. She shouldn't be moving at all. What if Lottie saw her?

But Lottie was more interested in finding something on the shelves near me. I pulled Ella back and we stood behind a large box, a girl's bicycle, hoping it would cover us from Lottie's sight. She was looking through the packages—too close to Victoria. Victoria looked right into my terrified eyes and somehow kept a Zen about her I could not have managed myself.

"You can ask for all the money you want. That doesn't mean you'll get anything." Lottie turned around suddenly and Ella and I ducked. I tugged at Ace's sleeve and he slowly crouched down near us, but he kept his eyes on Lottie.

Whatever she was looking for, she'd found it. The sound of shuffling through boxes ended and her footsteps stopped in front of the box where Ella and I were hiding. I held my breath and risked a peek. I ducked back. Lottie's arm protruded past the edge of the box. She was standing inches from us, pointing in the direction where I could see Noah was standing.

I looked to Hart, then Jones. They'd neared the end of the long rows but were hesitating to turn the corner. They'd have Lottie trapped in a minute, but only after she trapped herself into a jail sentence. They were waiting for some kind of admission of guilt, which Ace could capture on the recorder he was now setting on the shelf.

Head Over Heels

Lottie might not give Noah that long. His acting ability didn't cover the real fear in his voice as he asked, "What are you doing?"

I had to look, even if Lottie could see me. There was a bottle in her hand, a perfume bottle pointed at Noah's face. Another poisoned perfume, I assumed.

From the other side of the aisle, Victoria waved again. No, she wasn't waving. She was making a pushing motion, two arms in front of her and then pointing at me. I looked at the bicycle box.

Of course. It was perfect.

"Just alerting you to a defective product. You didn't think I'd only made one, did you?" said Lottie.

But before she could spray the poisonous substance, I pushed the box as hard as I could. With Ella's help, it finally budged. Lottie screamed and crashed onto the floor. I could see her heels slip from under her. Noah ducked out of the way of the bottle in case Lottie managed to spray it. Fortunately, she did not.

Hart and Jones darted forward, with Hart shouting, "Police! Stay on the ground."

But they were far enough away that she had time to move around Noah, using him as a shield.

"Come any closer and I'll spray him!" she threatened.

She could see Ella and me now, so she backed toward the opposite side of the aisles, unaware that Victoria was behind those shelves.

"Easy," Hart said.

He wasn't talking to Lottie. The rest of us could see Victoria's hand creeping behind Lottie's wrist. If she had any indication Victoria was there, she might pull away. I held my breath, hoping Victoria could grab Lottie's wrist before she had time to spray the poison.

She shot out, knocking over boxes and bottles in the process. Lottie cried out as Victoria twisted her wrist and her finger. The bottle slipped from Lottie's hand.

"Catch it!" I yelled.

Noah turned, hit the bottle clumsily, and ended up jettisoning it toward us. Ella gasped. I pulled her away, tucking her head down, away from the shelf, but I couldn't help but keep my eyes on the action.

Ace outpaced Hart, grabbing the perfume bottle in one swoop. Lottie broke free of Victoria and tried to dash away but it was too late.

Jones grappled with her arm. She wouldn't hold still until he'd wrestled her to the ground and he and Hart bound her wrists—including the one that was sprained, thanks to Victoria—into the handcuffs. Then, she let out a shriek of pain and frustration.

Head Over Heels

Hart tipped his head to me on one side and to Victoria on the other before turning his attention to Lottie. "You have the right to—"

"Don't tell me my rights, I already know them," Lottie snapped.

Ace handed the perfume to Hart and then walked over to me. Putting an arm on the shelf, he leaned toward me, saying, "I don't think I've ever seen Hart so impressed."

"That's impressed, is it?" I teased.

"Well, if it wasn't to him, it was to me."

Heat rose into my cheeks.

"I didn't mean to hurt her. I just wanted to stop her," I said.

Ace smiled at me in a way that deepened my blush. I had leaned in, too. We were inches apart between a basket of blush and a box of lipstick coincidentally stamped with a pair of glossy red lips. And we were only now just realizing we were so close. And so not alone.

Noah came over and stood right next to Ace, leaning over the shelf. I pulled back. Noah didn't seem to notice.

"I'm so glad you knocked that lady over. You saved my life," Noah said.

Lottie wasn't done. Though she couldn't fight back with fists, she could with words. Struggling against Officer Jones's grip, she raged at the sight of Victoria.

"It's not fair! I should have the successful company, not you. Tara should be working for me! You should have been working for me!"

"Everything I have I worked to get," Victoria said.

As if Victoria were toxic to her, Lottie doubled over. She fell to one knee and breathed hard. Jones clutched her arm and she leaned into him. I stepped forward.

"Officer Hart, she washed her lab coat so you wouldn't find it, but the poisoned perfume bottle leaked. She has arsenic in her system. It's slowly poisoning her."

Officer Hart nodded. To Jones, he said, "Call for a paramedic. Ace and I have her."

"I'm fine." Lottie struggled to stand.

Victoria reached out to Lottie, who looked up at her without accepting her hand. Without anger or malice, Victoria said, "The only difference between you and me is that I recognized and appreciated what life did give me: a chance. Despite what you did to LeBeau, no one here wants you dead. Take the help."

Lottie stood of her own accord, holding her head up high as the officers escorted her out.

The lack of guilt in Lottie's expression made me shudder. "Let's get out of here," I said.

"Agreed," Ella said. "And Kait?"

I turned and raised a brow.

Head Over Heels

Ella breathed in deep like the words were going to hurt. "You did a good job."

Chapter 13

A Turn on the Catwalk

Back in the storefront, Victoria, who did not make a habit of emotional displays, pulled me into an embrace so tight a corset would have been put to shame. When she finally let go, she was beaming. It was a shade more dazzling than any collection Victress carried: pure joy.

"You did it!" she said.

"Knocking over the box was your idea," I replied.

"Now I just have to spin the publicity to win back my customers. How about this for a headline? *"Victress was no victim to would-be character assassin and murderess Charlotte Hambledon."*

"Brilliant." Helen placed herself between Victoria and me. Pointing to the Victress Cosmetics sign, she asked, "Do I understand correctly that this your brand?"

Head Over Heels

Beaming, Victoria answered, "Yes, it is."

"Masterfully done." Helen held up a mirror and admired the reflection. Daisy blushed. The makeup may have been Victoria's, but the handiwork was Daisy's. And she'd done a stunning job. I'd never seen Helen so radiant.

Victoria's eyes narrowed on Helen. "I've seen you before."

Helen held out a hand. "Helen Teagan, modeling agent."

Victoria took her hand and Helen shook it with vigor. "There's a resort fashion show in two weeks and I think your brand is the best one for our models."

"Your agency deals with cosmetic brands?" Victoria raised an eyebrow.

"I know the designer and I'm sure he'd take my recommendation. Once you get this job, the whole world of fashion shows will be open to you." Helen flicked a card out of her fingers so fast one would think she was a magician. "Call me and we'll start making arrangements."

Victoria took the card. "Thank you, Miss Teagan. I'll do that." She marveled at the chic black and pink card with a simple name on the front, phone number on the back.

"I'm sorry I couldn't get you to model, Kait. But I'll be in touch."

"I'll be here," I replied.

When Helen had walked away, Victoria looked at me suspiciously. "You didn't arrange this, did you?" she asked in a tone that told me she didn't want any pity clients.

She didn't have to worry about that. I shook my head. "I may have given her a coupon for a makeover, but that's it."

I nudged Victoria. "You might need that team of makeup artists after all." I looked at Daisy.

Victoria's eyes fell on Daisy. "You did the makeover?"

Daisy nodded. "Of course, I used your brand, so it was easy to make her look good."

As if transforming into business mode right in front of my eyes, Victoria stepped toward Daisy, saying, "If you still want the job, I'd be happy to hire you."

Daisy nearly hugged Victoria but caught herself and turned it into a handshake. Letting go of Daisy's hand, Victoria looked over the counter. The wide array of Victress products on display was impressive.

Victoria remarked, "I'm grateful Coraline's is still using my brand after the accusations."

Head Over Heels

"There was a letter to Coraline's about the brand being checked for health and safety. It all checked out, so the store had no choice but to keep the product. Besides, Ella threatened to kick Coraline's out or sue if we discontinued the product."

I looked toward the store entrance where Ella was talking with Ace. For all I knew, she was still flirting, but this time her hands were not attached to his arms like a purse-snatcher to a Louis Vuitton. When she caught my eyes for a second, I smiled. She didn't return the look, of course, but there was a tiny nod I couldn't read. It may have been "good job" or "glad you're okay." Whatever it was, it was a start.

Victoria focused on a different part of Daisy's revelation. "I didn't send a letter. Noah?" She caught his attention from where he was a standing talking with Officer Jones. He walked over to hear her question. "Did you send our records of health and safety inspections to Coraline's?"

Noah's eyes widened. "No, I didn't." He smiled. "You know, Tara was the one who kept those records."

An awe fell over Victoria's face. She looked at the card in her hands, embarrassed by the blush rising in her cheeks. Victoria had always been embarrassed by extremes of emotions. At least this time, the emotion was happiness.

Chapter 14

A Thing of Beauty

I smoothed the fabric of my chiffon, floral, off-the-shoulder dress and walked confidently in my fuchsia heels to the front door. With my matching clutch in one hand, I kept adjusting the gold pin on my dress. I wasn't so much worried that it would tear the material as I was that it wouldn't be visible to my mystery man.

The door was partly open for the spring breeze, so I went on through. I could see a few guests on the other side of the sliding doors in the backyard, but it was hard to tell if any of them were my intended date. I couldn't believe the way my heart was racing. I needed a deep breath before stepping farther inside.

A chuckling to my right stopped me. I turned to see a gentleman in a periwinkle shirt and gray pants. He was just putting on his tie, looking at the mirror in the entryway. Although he hadn't turned around yet, he had seen me through the mirror.

"Oh, Ace, it's you. Happy Birthday," I said, handing him the gift.

"Thank you." He took the present and set it on the bench. Then he leaned down to swing his suit jacket over his shoulders.

"You look nice."

"You say that like you're surprised."

"No, it's just, the suit and tie is a little more formal than I thought you'd be."

"I'd say the same about you, but you're always fashionable. I do have a reason, though. I'm supposed to be meeting a blind date today."

"Really? That's a coincidence, I was—wait, here at your birthday party?"

A feminine voice called out from the hallway, "Okay, Aeson, I'm free for a second. You needed help with a pin or something?"

Ace's sister stepped into the room dressed in a yellow blouse and a pair of capri pants. She smiled when she saw me. "Kait! I'm so glad you're here."

Head Over Heels

"I wouldn't have missed it for anything," I said as she pulled me into a hug, but my mind was still on Ace. And so were my eyes.

Maisie picked up on my distraction. Looking between Ace and me, she stepped aside.

"Maybe Kait can help you with...whatever it was. I'll just go see if everyone is set outside."

As she stepped away, I stepped closer. "Who set you up on this blind date?"

He pulled a gold rose pin out of his jacket pocket and held it out to me.

"Who do you think?"

"Scarlett," I said with a hint of *I should have known* in my voice.

"Well, you don't have to sound so angry about it."

"I'm not." I relaxed into a smile. "I'm just wondering what Scarlett was thinking. I mean, you are my boss, after all."

"That's true." He chuckled again.

"This is funny to you?" Part of me agreed that it was humorous, and the other part disliked being manipulated—no matter how well-intentioned the person was in pulling my heartstrings.

"I had a feeling it was you. Scarlett isn't as hard to read as she thinks. She was talking about you long before you moved here, in fact."

Now that he mentioned it, I remembered that Scarlett had been the one who gave me Ace's card when I first came to Diamond Springs. She'd insisted on me hiring him when Ava had been accused of murder. Then, of course, there was Scarlett's own admission that she'd tried to set us up the summer I'd graduated from boarding school.

"Seems like she's been trying to play matchmaker for us for a while now." I grinned. It was strange how life worked out. Ace and I had become partners, even if it wasn't how Scarlett had pictured. That thought sparked worry. "This isn't going to work, though, is it?"

A little more hope intruded in my voice than I wanted to show. Did he know that I was secretly hoping he'd say that he wanted it to work? That he felt the same spark between all our quips and quarrels? Or worse, did he know how crushed I'd feel if he didn't feel the same way? If I couldn't keep the hope hidden, I wanted to at least keep the dejected tone out of my voice if he turned me down. I readied myself for rejection.

Ace smiled with no hint of worry, no mixed feelings, or hesitation. Taking my hand, he wrapped our arms together and walked with me through the house. I felt butterflies in my stomach as we passed the kitchen. He opened the sliding door to join the others under the clear skies of a sunny day. But before we stepped over the threshold, he stopped.

His gray eyes pierced mine with an intensity that I'd never seen. It was no wonder how he could unravel a suspect with that look. My defenses came undone as I gazed into his eyes. In the most gentlemanly of gestures, his lips brushed my hand with a light kiss.

Ace said, "I'm not crossing us off my list of possibilities."

The smoldering look growing in his eyes gave me goosebumps, even though the weather was heating up. All I could think as I walked through the door to join our friends was that I had better be careful. If he kept looking at me like that, I might fall head over heels.

Want more great content?

Hi, I'm Astoria Wright, the author of A Sassy Sleuth's Mystery series. I hope you've enjoyed Book 2: Head Over Heels.

Check out the rest of
A Sassy Sleuth's Mystery series:
Hot on the Heels
Head Over Heels
Heels Dug In

Check out Astoria Wright's other series,
the Faerie Apothecary Mysteries:
Chaos in the Countryside
Herbs and Homicide
Remedy and Ruins
Elixirs and Elves
Charms and Changelings
Potions and Panic
Talismans and Turmoil
Tonics and Turning Points

To keep up-to-date about this series and others by the author, check out the website:

www.astoriawright.com

Sign up for the mailing list for updates and freebies available only to members!

Thanks for reading!

www.ingramcontent.com/pod-product-compliance
Lightning Source LLC
Chambersburg PA
CBHW020140150626
46552CB00021B/847